DUMP TRUCK DUCK

MEGAN E. BRYANT

pictures by
JO DE RUITER

ALBERT WHITMAN & COMPANY
CHICAGO, ILLINOIS

Rumble, rumble, hear that truck?

At the wheel is Dump Truck Duck!

On his way to the great big dig,

honking as he steers his rig.

The site is where he'll work all day,
clearing hunks of junk away.
Making room for other trucks
driven by some other ducks.

He fills the truck up to the top
with gravel, grass, and gritty glop;
with brambly brush and slimy stuff.
The truck can take it. The truck is tough.

Soon Dozer Duck and Digger Duck
drive their trucks right through the muck.
The track wheels turn, the dirt road shakes
from grinding gears and screeching brakes.

With their vests and hard hats on,
ducks dig up the scrubby lawn.
Clouds of dust and dirt appear
as the site begins to clear.

Pull that lever, Dozer Duck!

Drive that dirt up to the truck.

Who can move this muddy mound?

And haul it over grubby ground?

A webby foot steps on the gas,

as Dump Truck Duck roars through the grass.

Scoops of dirt soar through the air—
see how Digger chucks them there?
Splat! They fall into the truck
and sometimes fall on Dump Truck Duck!
A whistle blows when there's enough.
The truck can take it. The truck is tough.

**Bumping, bouncing down the road,
ready for another load.**

He honks the horn and calls out, "Quack!"
Then Dump Truck Duck drives right on back.

Whoa! What was that awful sound?
Something crunches on the ground.
The big truck shudders to a stop.
Dump Truck Duck pops up the top
and takes a look beneath the hood.
The truck's not working like it should.

Once the smoke has cleared away,
he understands the big delay.
An engine jammed with thorns and twigs
can't keep up with other rigs.

One by one, the ducks must pluck
prickly stickers that got stuck.
The work is hard. The work is rough.
But ducks can take it. Ducks are tough!

The three truck ducks will all high-five
when the builder ducks arrive.
Gardener ducks lay out some sod,
root by root and clod by clod.

At last the long day's work is done—
a new park sparkles in the sun!

The ducks are tired; the ducks are proud.
They smile at the happy crowd.

Then dirty ducks jump in the creek
to wash each feather, foot, and beak.
They flap their wings; they dive and dip.
They belly flop and triple flip!

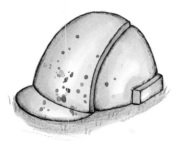

Ducks load their trucks and hop inside,
buckling up for a bumpy ride.

As the stars shine through the night,
they dream of new construction sites.
A bridge, a road, a brand-new nest...
building is what ducks do best!

For my ducklings, Clara and Sam, with truckloads of love–MB

For Patch, a very keen duck feeder!–JDR

Library of Congress Cataloging-in-Publication
data is on file with the publisher.

Text copyright © 2016 by Megan E. Bryant
Pictures copyright © 2016 by Albert Whitman & Company
Pictures by Jo de Ruiter
Published in 2016 by Albert Whitman & Company
ISBN 978-0-8075-1736-9

Printed in China
10 9 8 7 6 5 4 3 2 1 LP 24 23 22 21 20 19 18 17 16 15

Design by Jordan Kost

For more information about Albert Whitman & Company,
visit our web site at www.albertwhitman.com.